THE GIANT ZUCCHINI

CATHERINE SIRACUSA

Hyperion Books for Children
New York

Printed in Italy. For more information address
Hyperion Books for Children,
114 Fifth Avenue, New York, New York 10011.

FIRST EDITION

1   3   5   7   9   10   8   6   4   2

Library of Congress Cataloging-in-Publication Data

Siracusa, Catherine.
The giant zucchini/Catherine Siracusa—1st ed.
p.   cm.
Summary: Edgar Mouse and Robert Squirrel grow a zucchini for the
county fair, not knowing that it has magic powers when they sing to it.
ISBN 1-56282-286-1 (trade)—ISBN 1-56282-287-X (lib. bdg.)
[1. Zucchini—Fiction.   2. Fairs—Fiction.   3. Magic—Fiction.
4. Mice—Fiction.   5. Squirrels—Fiction.]   I. Title.
PZ7.S6215Gi   1993
[E]—dc20
92-72018   CIP   AC

The artwork for each picture is prepared using gouache,
watercolors, pencil, and colored pencils.

This book is set in 18-point Goudy Old Style.

To Uncle Bill, Uncle Dante,
Uncle Erny, and Aunt Isabelle
—C. S.

Edgar Mouse was in his garden.

"It is getting late," he said.

"Where is Robert?"

Just then Robert Squirrel

drove up in his truck.

"I am back!" said Robert.

"What took you so long?" asked Edgar.

"Did you get the zucchini seeds?"

"I got something better," said Robert.

"It was on sale."

"What is it?" asked Edgar.

"It is a zucchini seed," said Robert.

"Only one?" asked Edgar.

"It is so heavy!"

"It is a giant zucchini," said Robert.

"What will we do

with a giant zucchini?"

Edgar asked.

"We can win first prize
at the county fair," said Robert.
"I never won anything before,"
said Edgar.
"It is our big chance," said Robert.
"Let's plant it right now!" said Edgar.

Edgar and Robert planted the seed
right in the middle of the garden.

They worked in their garden
every day.
They weeded and watered.
They made a scarecrow.

They even put up a tent
and slept there every night.
"I wish the giant zucchini
would hurry up and grow,"
said Robert.
"Do not worry," said Edgar.
"It takes time."

One day the giant zucchini sprouted.

"It will not be long now!" said Edgar.

It blossomed a little bit.

And a little zucchini began to grow.

Soon it was time for the county fair.

"Our giant zucchini is not very big," said Robert.

"Did we do something wrong?"

"I am sure we did everything right," Edgar said.

"But this is not a giant zucchini. It is a teeny zucchini!"

"I should never have bought that seed on sale," said Robert.

"Maybe we can win the prize for the teeniest," said Edgar.

"Maybe we can," said Robert.

"Let's go to the fair!"

Edgar sat in the back of Robert's truck
with the teeny zucchini.
On the way to the county fair,
big trucks passed them
carrying big carrots,
big cabbages, big onions,
and other big vegetables.

"This is awful," said Edgar.

"Cheer up!" said Robert.

"Sing us a song while I drive."

"I am too sad to sing," said Edgar.

Just then a big hog in a big truck

tried to run them off the road.

"Get out of my way!"

shouted the hog.

"Road hog!" cried Robert.

In the back of the hog's truck

was a giant zucchini.

"It is gigantic!" said Robert.

"Our zucchini is so teeny," said Edgar.

Then Edgar began to sing,

Teeny zucchini,
Teeny and small,
I wish you'd grow big,
The biggest of all!

"I will sing, too!" said Robert.

When they sang together,

the teeny zucchini began to grow.

"It is getting bigger!" said Edgar.

"Let's keep singing!" cried Robert.

17

The teeny zucchini grew and grew

as Edgar and Robert sang and sang.

"Are you humming, Robert?"

"No," said Robert. "Are you?"

Hummm!

"It is the zucchini!

It is humming our song,"

said Edgar.

"It is magic!" said Robert.

Hummm!

By the time they got to the fair,

the teeny zucchini

was a giant zucchini!

The giant zucchini rolled

off Robert's truck.

It rolled down a hill.

"Wait for us!" cried Edgar and Robert.

They followed the giant zucchini

down the hill and into a tent.

The tent flap opened.

"There is that hog

who tried to run us off the road,"

whispered Robert.

The hog pulled his giant zucchini
into the tent.

"Who are you?" said the hog
to Edgar and Robert.

"I am Edgar Mouse and this is
my friend Robert Squirrel," said Edgar.

"And this is our giant zucchini,"
said Robert.

"We are going to win first prize."

"You must be kidding," said the hog.

"I am Humphrey Hog,
the zucchini champion.
My giant zucchinis
always win first prize."

"Not this time," said Robert.

Humphrey measured their zucchini
from end to end.
He poked it and prodded it.
"Eek!" said the giant zucchini.
"Did you say something?"
said Humphrey to Edgar.

"I did not say anything,"
said Edgar.

Humphrey smiled sweetly.

"Your giant zucchini *is* bigger
than mine," he said.

"I knew we would win!" said Robert.

"The judge will not be here
until three o'clock," said Humphrey.
"You two should go
and enjoy the fair."

"I think we should stay
with our zucchini," said Edgar.
"I will take care of your zucchini,"
said Humphrey.

Humphrey handed some free passes
to Robert and Edgar.

"The fun is on me," said Humphrey.

"Thank you, Humphrey," said Robert.

"Come on, Edgar. Let's have some fun!"

"Thank you," said Edgar.

"See you later, zucchini!"

Robert and Edgar rode the Ferris wheel
and the merry-go-round.
They played games and ate popcorn,
peanuts, and cotton candy.

Edgar looked at his watch.

"Let's go back to our zucchini," he said.

"You worry too much," said Robert.

"But we can go back if you want."

Robert and Edgar walked

back to the tent.

But their giant zucchini

was not there.

"It is gone!" cried Edgar.

"Is something wrong?" asked Humphrey.

"What happened to our giant zucchini?"

asked Edgar.

Humphrey patted his zucchini.

"This is the only giant zucchini

at the fair," he said.

"You stole it!" cried Robert.

"You are mistaken. I have
never seen you or your zucchini,"
said Humphrey.

"But you gave us free passes,"
said Edgar.

"Come on, Robert, let's go," said Edgar.

"But Humphrey is lying!" said Robert.

"Soon it will be three o'clock,"
said Edgar. "We have to find
our zucchini."

"It is so big," said Robert.

"It will not be hard to find."

Robert and Edgar ran through the fair.

They searched everywhere.

"It must be here somewhere,"

said Edgar.

"Let's climb that haystack," said Robert.

"Then we can see the whole fair."

Robert and Edgar climbed

to the top of the haystack.

Their giant zucchini

was nowhere to be seen.

"It is all my fault," said Robert.

"No, it is not," said Edgar. "It is my fault.

Let's sing a song. Maybe that will help."

Edgar and Robert sang very loud,

Zucchini, zucchini,

Oh, where did you go?

Dear giant zucchini,

Please hum so we'll know!

They sang the song over and over.

Suddenly the haystack began to shake.

"It is an earthquake!" cried Robert.

Then they heard a loud hum.

"Our zucchini is here!" cried Edgar.

"It is under the hay!" cried Robert.

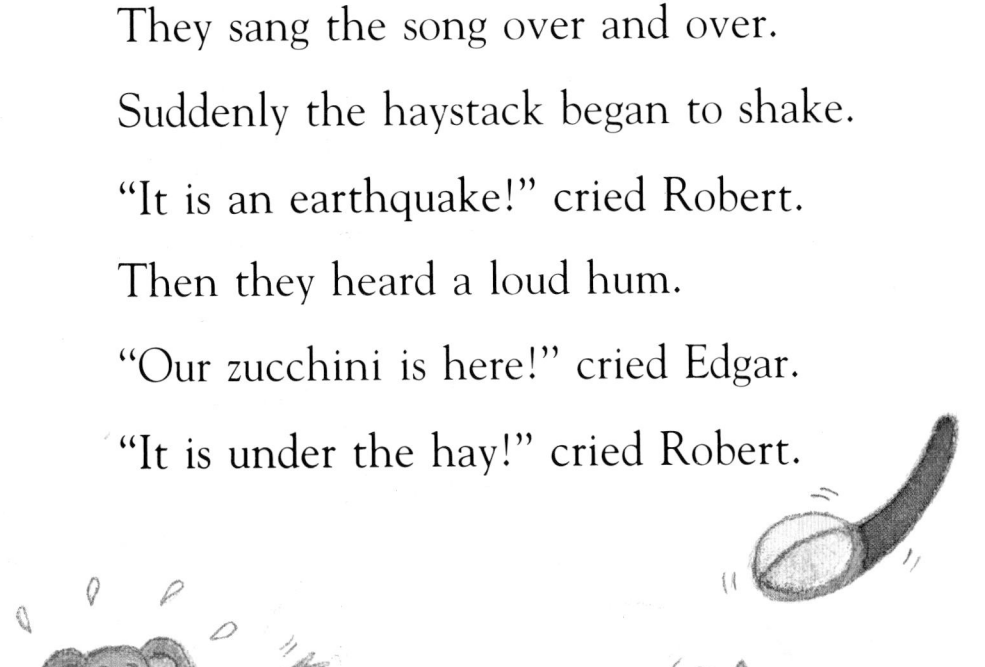

Robert and Edgar dug through the hay
until they found their zucchini.

"How did you get here?" asked Edgar.

"Hum!" said the giant zucchini.

"Hum-phrey!"

"I knew it," cried Robert.

Hum-phrey!

Hummmmmmm!

"We will never get back to the tent
by three o'clock," said Edgar.
"If only we could fly."
The giant zucchini hummed.
"Let's sing a flying song," said Robert.
"Our zucchini can do anything."

39

They sang,

Zucchini, zucchini,

So green and so wise,

Let's fly to the tent

And win the first prize!

The giant zucchini lifted up

out of the hay.

Then it hummed and took off.

"Hang on tight!" cried Edgar.

The giant zucchini flew over the fair.

Hummmmm!

It flew into the tent.

The judge was just about to give

the blue ribbon to Humphrey Hog.

"Wait!" shouted Edgar and Robert.

"HUMMM!" said the giant zucchini.

"Wow!" said the judge.

"It is huge! It flies! It hums!"

He handed the blue ribbon

to Edgar and Robert.

"That belongs to me!" said Humphrey.

"Not this time," said the judge.

Humphrey tried to grab the blue ribbon.

The giant zucchini

rolled onto his foot.

"Ouch!" shouted Humphrey.

"Remove this hog at once!"
said the judge.

A police officer pulled Humphrey
out of the tent.

"Humphrey is not used to losing,"
said the judge.

"Your giant zucchini
is the most amazing one
I have ever seen or heard.
How did you grow it?" he asked.

"We sing to it," said Edgar and Robert.

Then they sang this song:

O teeny zucchini,

We sang and you grew.

Dear giant zucchini,

We sang and you flew!

Zucchini, zucchini,

So green and so wise,

You flew through the air

And won the first prize!